THE BUS FOR US

Suzanne Bloom

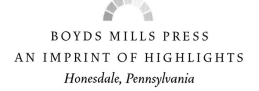

BOYDS MILLS PRESS

AN IMPRINT OF HIGHLIGHTS

Honesdale, Pennsylvania

Boyds Mills Press, Inc.
An Imprint of Highlights
815 Church Street
Honesdale, Pennsylvania 18431
Printed in China

Library of Congress Cataloging-in-Publication Data

Bloom, Suzanne.
    The bus for us / written and illustrated by Suzanne Bloom.—1st ed.
 [32]p. : col. ill. ; cm.
Summary: On her first day of school, Tess wonders what the school bus
will look like.
 ISBN: 978-1-56397-932-3 (hc) • ISBN: 978-1-62091-441-0 (pb)
1. School — Fiction. 2. School buses — Fiction. I. Title.
 [E] 21 2001 AC CIP
00-102348

First edition
The text of this book is set in Palatino.

10 9 8 7 6 5

To four fabulous first-grade teachers and to Alice, who always asked
—SB

"Is this the bus for us, Gus?"

"No, Tess. This is a taxi."

BUS
STOP

"Is this the bus for us, Gus?"

"No, Tess. This is a tow truck."

"Is this the bus for us, Gus?"

"No, Tess. This is a fire engine."

"Is this the bus for us, Gus?"

"No, Tess. This is an ice-cream truck."

"Is this the bus for us, Gus?"

"No, Tess. This is a garbage truck."

"Is this the bus for us, Gus?"

"No, Tess. This is a backhoe."

"Is this the bus for us, Gus?"

"Yes, Tess. This is the bus for us. Let's go!"

When her sons were younger, Suzanne Bloom
waited with them for their school bus each day. She
is the author and illustrator of the picture books
featuring Goose and Bear: *A Splendid Friend, Indeed*,
selected as a Theodor Seuss Geisel Honor Book
by the American Library Association; *Treasure*;
What About Bear?; and *Oh! What a Surprise!*
Some of her other books include *Feeding
Friendsies*, *No Place for a Pig*, *A Mighty Fine Time
Machine*, and *We Keep a Pig in the Parlor*. She is also
the illustrator of *Girls: A to Z* and *My Special Day at
Third Street School*, both by Eve Bunting, and *Melissa
Parkington's Beautiful, Beautiful Hair* by Pat Brisson,
winner of the Paterson Prize for Books for Young
People (Special Recognition). She lives with her
family in McDonough, New York.